4-22

Mom, There's a Bear at the Door

Written by

Sabine Lipan

Illustrated by

Manuela Olten

EERDMANS BOOKS FOR YOUNG READERS

GRAND RAPIDS, MICHIGAN / CAMBRIDGE, U.K.

First published in the United States in 2016 by
Eerdmans Books for Young Readers,
an imprint of Wm. B. Eerdmans Publishing Co.
2140 Oak Industrial Dr. NE
Grand Rapids, Michigan 49505
P.O. Box 163, Cambridge CB3 9PU U.K.

www.eerdmans.com/youngreaders

Originally published in Germany in 2014 under the title
Mama, da steht ein Bär vor der Tür!
by Tulipan Verlag GmbH, München, Germany

Text by Sabine Lipan
Illustrations by Manuela Olten
© 2014 Tulipan Verlag GmbH
English language translation provided by Tulipan Verlag
and edited by Eerdmans Books for Young Readers
This English edition © Eerdmans Books for Young Readers

Manufactured at Tien Wah Press in Malaysia

22 21 20 19 18 17 16   9 8 7 6 5 4 3 2 1

ISBN 978-0-8028-5460-5

A catalog listing is available from the Library of Congress.

The illustrations were created using acrylic paint and colored pencil.
The display type was set in Mom's Diner.
The text type was set in Thonburi.

FSC
www.fsc.org

MIX
Paper from
responsible sources
FSC® C012700

Mom, there's a bear at the door!

A bear?

A bear.

But we live on the eleventh floor!

That's why he's there.

How did the bear get up here?

He took the elevator.

The elevator?

The elevator.

The bear pressed the button and took the elevator?

Of course! The elevator doesn't work if no one presses the button.

And how did the bear get to the city?

He took the bus. How else?

He took the bus?

He took the bus.

The bear had a ticket?

He probably bought one.

The bear bought a ticket?

He's not allowed to get on
the bus without a ticket!
So he must have bought one.

And how did the bear get to the bus stop?

He rode his bicycle.

His bicycle?

His bicycle.

The bear has a bicycle?

He has to have one if he rode it!

The bear can ride a bicycle?

Otherwise he couldn't have gotten from his forest to the bus stop.

The bear came from the forest?

All bears come from the forest!

This one too?

This one too.

And where is there a forest
in the middle of the city?

**There has to be one. Otherwise the
bear wouldn't have come here.**

And what does the bear want, here on our eleventh floor?

To look at the sea.

At the sea?

At the sea.

The bear from the forest wants to look out at the sea, here in the middle of the city?

Yes, he can't see it in that thick forest.

And how will he look at it from here?

Through the window. How else?

And when he has seen the sea, he'll leave?

Not until he's had lunch.

What does the bear eat, exactly?

Black Forest cake. And honey cake.

Black Forest cake?

Black Forest cake.

And honey cake?

Yes, both. There's nobody to bake for him in the forest.

And then when he has seen the sea and eaten the Black Forest cake and the honey cake, then he will go back to his forest?

Exactly.

First he'll take the elevator down?

First he'll take the elevator down.

And then he'll take the bus to the edge of the forest?
Then he'll take the bus to the edge of the forest.

And then he'll ride his bike back to his cave?

Then he'll ride his bike back to his cave.

And then?

Then he'll go to sleep. Of course. The bear will be tired after such a long day!

Manuela Olten studied children's book illustration at the Offenbach University of Art and Design. Her debut picture book, *Boys Are Best* (Boxer), received the Oldenburg Children's Book Prize in Germany and was also nominated for the German Youth Literature Prize. She lives in Germany.